Choi, Sook Nyul.

Halmoni and the
    picnic.

$16.00

Halmoni and the Picnic

Sook Nyul Choi

Illustrated by Karen M. Dugan

Houghton Mifflin Company
Boston

Library of Congress Cataloging-in-Publication Data

Choi, Sook Nyul.
  Halmoni and the picnic / Sook Nyul Choi ; illustrated by Karen
M. Dugan
    p.   cm.
  Summary: A Korean American girl's third grade class helps her
newly arrived grandmother feel more comfortable with her new life in
the United States.
  ISBN 0-395-61626-3
  [1. Korean Americans — Fiction. 2. Grandmothers — Fiction.]
  I. Milone-Dugan, Karen, ill. II. Title.
  PZ7.C44626Ha1   1993   91-34121
  [E] — dc20   CIP
                                 AC

Printed in the United States of America

WOZ   10   9   8   7

To my daughters, Kathleen and Audrey
and
To my editor, Laura Hornik

—S.N.C.

Hand in hand, Yunmi and her grandmother, Halmoni, walked toward St. Patrick's Elementary School. Taxi cabs darted between the big buses rumbling down busy Fourteenth Street. Yunmi squeezed Halmoni's hand and smiled. Halmoni nodded in acknowledgment, but kept her eyes on the street without smiling. Just like the day before, Halmoni looked sad as they drew closer to the school. She did not like going back to their empty apartment all alone.

Miss Stein, in her white uniform, was coming back from working the night shift at Beth Israel Hospital.

"Good morning, Miss Stein!" Yunmi called.

"Oh, hello, Yunmi," said Miss Stein, half smiling and half yawning.

"Yunmi," Halmoni said in Korean, "you must not call out to grown-ups. You should lower your eyes out of respect. It is rude for little ones to disturb their elders!"

Yunmi giggled. "Halmoni, people like it when I greet them. In America it isn't rude to call grown-ups by their names. Here it is rude *not* to say hello and *not* to look people in the eye when you speak to them."

Halmoni sighed. "I will never get used to living here."

Yunmi was sad for her grandmother, who found America too different from Korea.

"Halmoni," she said, "my friends like the bags of fruit you give them each morning."

"I am glad. It is always nice to share with friends," said Halmoni.

"Will you please say hello to my friends in English this morning? They will be so surprised to hear you talk to them. I know you can. Please, Halmoni?"

Halmoni replied, "No, I have only been here for two months. English words are still too difficult for my old tongue. I will sound funny. I will give them this fruit; that is my way of saying hello to them. Besides, you do enough talking for both of us!"

"Yunmi, Yunmi, wait for me!" they heard Anna Marie shout from behind them.

Then Helen came running up from a side street. "Hi, Anna Marie! Hi, Yunmi!"

They said hello to Halmoni. Halmoni nodded and gave one brown bag to each girl.

"Oh, thank you!" said Helen.

"Goody," said Anna Marie. "An apple, grapes, and cherries, too!" The girls said goodbye to Halmoni and headed toward the school yard.

Helen said, "Yunmi, your grandmother is so nice, but she never says anything. Why don't you teach her some English?"

Yunmi shook her head sadly. "My grandmother is embarrassed to speak with an accent. She could speak English if she wanted to. She is smart. She used to be a teacher in Korea."

Helen thought for a while. "Maybe your grandmother is not happy here. When I'm not happy, I don't want to learn anything new. Maybe she's like me."

"That's true. I'm like that, too," Anna Marie agreed.

Yunmi sighed just like Halmoni and said, "I think she's lonely when I'm at school. My parents are so busy working that they have no time for her. I know she misses her old friends, but I don't want her to go back to Korea."

"She needs new friends!" Anna Marie exclaimed. "We can be her friends. We see her every day and we like her."

"We must do something to show her that we want to be her new friends," Helen said with determination. "What can we do?"

They entered the school yard and sat under the big oak tree thinking quietly. That morning they did not play tag or jump rope. When the bell rang, they went to their classroom and unpacked their bookbags in silence.

13

"Children, I have a special announcement to make this morning," Mrs. Nolan said. "Next Tuesday is our annual picnic in Central Park. We need a chaperon, so please ask your parents if one of them can come and help us."

Helen and Anna Marie raised their arms high, nearly falling off their chairs. Surprised, Mrs. Nolan said, "Yes, Helen, you first. What is it?"

Helen blushed, then asked, "Can Yunmi's grandmother be our chaperon, please?"

Mrs. Nolan said, "Of course. But Yunmi must ask her grandmother first. Will you, Yunmi?"

Helen and Anna Marie grinned and nodded at Yunmi with excitement. But Yunmi was suddenly confused and worried. What if Halmoni did not want to come? What if the children made fun of her pointed rubber shoes and her long Korean dress?

That afternoon Yunmi cautiously told Halmoni what had happened at school.

Halmoni blushed with pleasure. "Helen said that? Your teacher wants me?"

So relieved to see Halmoni looking happy, Yunmi nodded her head up and down.

Touching Yunmi's cheek, Halmoni asked, "And do you want me to go to the picnic with you?"

"Yes, yes, Halmoni, it will be fun. You will meet all my friends, and Mrs. Nolan, and we will be together all day long in Central Park."

"Then yes, I will come," Halmoni said.

Halmoni would not go to the picnic empty-handed. She prepared a huge fruit basket for the third graders. She also insisted on making large plates of kimbap and a big jug of barley tea. Kimbap is made of rice, carrots, eggs, and green vegetables wrapped in seaweed. Again, Yunmi was worried. Most of the children would bring bologna or peanut butter sandwiches, which they would wash down with soda pop. What if no one wanted to eat Halmoni's kimbap? What if they made faces?

"Halmoni, please do not take the kimbap to the picnic. It took you so long to make. Let's save it for us to eat later."

"Oh, it was no problem. It looks so pretty and it's perfect for picnics. I wonder if I made enough."

On the morning of the picnic, Yunmi and her grandmother met the bus at school. Halmoni wore her pale blue skirt and top, called a ch'ima and chogori in Korean, with her white socks and white pointed rubber shoes.

When they arrived at Central Park, Halmoni sat under a big chestnut tree and watched the children play. The children took off their jackets and threw them in front of Halmoni. Smiling, she picked them up, shook off the grass and dirt, and folded each of them neatly. She liked the cool earth beneath her and the ringing laughter of the children.

At lunchtime, Halmoni placed the plates of kimbap on a large blue and white silk table cloth. Mrs. Nolan came over and gasped. "Oh, how beautiful they look! Children, come over and look at this. Yunmi's grandmother made my favorite lunch." Halmoni gave Mrs. Nolan a pair of chopsticks and poured a bit of soy sauce into a small dish. As the children munched on their sandwiches, they gathered around and watched Mrs. Nolan pop the little pieces of kimbap into her mouth.

Halmoni picked up one kimbap with her chopsticks and held it out to Helen. "Mogobwa," she said, which means "Try it." Helen understood and opened her mouth. Everyone watched her expression carefully as she chewed the strange-looking food. Her cautious chewing turned to delight. "Ummm, it's good!"

Then, Halmoni picked up another one and held
it out for Anna Marie. "Nodo," she said, which means
"You too." Anna Marie chewed slowly and then her
face brightened, too. Helen and Anna Marie were
ready for seconds, and soon everyone was eating the
kimbap.

Halmoni smiled, displaying all her teeth. She forgot
that in Korea it is not dignified for a woman to smile
in public without covering her mouth with her hand.

After lunch, some children asked Halmoni to hold one end of their jump rope. Others asked if Halmoni would make kimbap again for next year's picnic. When Yunmi translated, Halmoni nodded and said, "Kurae, kurae," meaning "Yes, yes."

The children started to chant as they jumped rope:

> "One, two, pointed shoe.
> Three, four, kimbap more.
> Five, six, chopsticks.
> Seven, eight, kimbap plate.
> Kurae, kurae, Picnic Day!"

Halmoni smiled until tears clouded her vision. Her long blue ch'ima danced in the breeze as she turned the jump rope. She tapped her shoes to the rhythm of their song.

Mrs. Nolan asked Yunmi, "What should the class call your grandmother? Mrs. Lee?"

Yunmi said, "I just call her Halmoni, which means grandmother. In Korea, it is rude to call elders by their names."

Mrs. Nolan nodded and smiled. "Children, why don't we all thank Halmoni for her delicious kimbap?"

"Thank you for the kimbap, Halmoni!" the children shouted in unison. Halmoni's wrinkled face turned red and she looked down at her pointed shoes. She took a handkerchief from the large sleeve of her chogori and wiped her eyes.

Halmoni was deep in thought as the big bus wove through the New York City streets. When the bus arrived back at school, the children hurried off, shouting goodbye. Halmoni murmured in English, "Goodbye, goodbye."

Filled with pride, Yunmi grabbed Halmoni's hand and gave it a squeeze. Halmoni squeezed back. Yunmi grinned, thinking of Halmoni's big smile as the children sang about her in Central Park. Skipping along Fourteenth Street, Yunmi hummed the kimbap song.

She thought she heard Halmoni quietly humming along, too.